THE CAVE

Kate Mosse

LARGE
PRINT

First published in 2009 by
Orion Books
This Large Print edition published
2009 by BBC Audiobooks by
arrangement with
the Author

ISBN 978 1 405 62267 7

British Library Cataloguing in Publication Data available

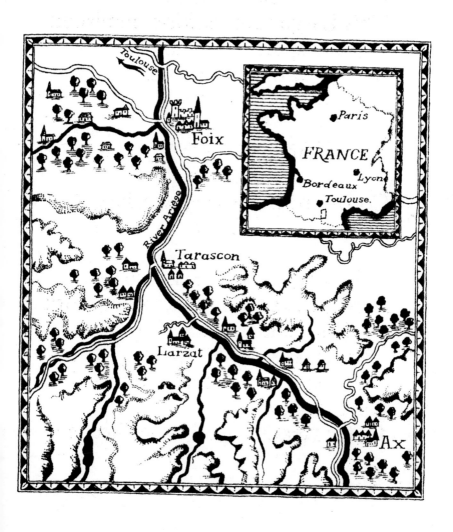

The past

April 1328

Now I see just bone and shadows. I see grief in the dust, in the darkness.

I am the last. The others all are dead. The old and the young have all slipped into darkness. Their souls have gone to a better place than this. At least, I pray that is true.

The end is coming. I welcome it. It has been a slow death, a living death, trapped here, inside this cave. It became our tomb. One by one, every heart stopped beating—my mother, my father, my brother. Now the only sounds are my shallow breathing and the gentle dripping of water down the walls of the cave. It is as if the mountain itself is weeping. As if it is mourning the dead.

During the long years of war, these tunnels gave us shelter. It was an underground city lit only by candles and torches. They kept us safe from the swords of those who hated us, from the broken bones, the torture, the ordeal of fire. Deep in the belly of the mountain, it was never too hot, never too cold. We only left at night, when blackness covered the mountains and the soldiers were sleeping. Only then did I feel the soft air on my cheeks and the wind in my hair.

These are the last words I will write. It will not be long now. I can no longer move my legs. My body does not obey me.

I think of the village where I grew up. I remember the snow that covered the upper fields from November to March every year. I remember the blue and pink and yellow flowers in spring. I remember swimming in the streams and the river, ice-cold from the melt-water that came down from the highest peaks. I remember the bleating of the sheep at the end of every summer day, the warm smell of freshly baked bread and the rattle of the wooden spinning wheels in the square. I remember the ringing of the single bell in the little church tower and how, at dusk each day, the sun came down to earth.

It is a place of ghosts now. The village is empty. The grass has grown wild around the front door of our house. The trees have grown tall in the square. The stone well where the women washed the clothes lies empty.

My last candle has burned out. I have passed too many days and nights in this cave without food and without water. My fingers are stiff and crooked, but I cannot stop writing. If one day the cave is opened and our bodies are found, I want the world to know our story, to understand who we were and why we died. To lay our bodies in the cold earth with a headstone and flowers at our grave. So we are not forgotten.

I do not fear death, though, even after all that happened, I will be sad to leave this life. In these last moments, all I hope is that this record of mine will be found, and that, on a distant day, my words will be read. When all else is done, only words remain. Words endure.

It is done. May God have mercy on my soul.

Marie of Larzat April 1328

Six hundred years later

April 1928

Chapter One

There was no doubt about it. He was lost.

Frederick Smith glanced at the map book lying on the passenger seat and frowned. If only he had stuck to the main road. He pulled the car over, took off his driving gloves and tried to work out exactly where he was.

He had not seen anyone else for some time. The pale rock of the mountain loomed above the valley. The hillside was covered with ancient woods. The road was a thin strip of grey, winding up, up into the distance.

Freddie was a pleasant-looking young man with freckles and sand-coloured hair. He had an open, trusting look and his mouth was fixed in a half-smile that made him seem simple. In fact, he was thoughtful, engaging, even though he had lost interest in life.

Freddie traced the route he had taken on the map with his finger, trying to work out where he had gone wrong. The brittle paper creaked and cracked under his touch.

He had set out from the French town of Foix where he had spent the night, after a good breakfast of fresh coffee, warm white rolls and butter. He had decided to take a detour and go by the mountain road. He hoped the views would lift his spirits, restore him. He wanted to enjoy life again. It had been a long time since anything much mattered.

At first all had gone well and Freddie had enjoyed the drive. It was a beautiful landscape, a place of wild contrasts—the splendour of the mountains ahead, the green beauty of the river valleys and gorges, the endless chill blue sky, the river running alongside. On the plains,

10

row after row of grapes on the vine stretched as far as the eye could see and there were olive trees with their silver-green leaves and black fruit. On the terraces of the houses, he saw earth-coloured pots filled with white and pink geraniums and blooms the size of a man's hand.

As he drove south, following the line of the river, he saw villages hidden in the folds of the mountains. On every peak stood the remains of a long-deserted fortress. Freddie knew the region had a terrible and bloody history. In the Middle Ages these silent, still plains and valleys had been the setting for more than a hundred years of war. The echoes of the past were everywhere.

The south-west of France had suffered less than the north-east in the recent war that had torn Europe apart. Even so, Freddie noticed that in every village there were monuments recording the names of all those who had died fighting for their country.

Freddie's brother George had gone to war and never come back. Missing in action in July 1917, presumed dead, his body had never been found. Even now, more than ten years on, Freddie still found it hard to believe George wouldn't stroll in the door one day. He thought he heard him whistling. Or he imagined him sitting in the old armchair blowing smoke rings.

Freddie took off his flat cap and ran his fingers over his oiled hair, smoothing it flat. After hours of jolting and rattling over stones and potholes, all he wanted was a long, hot bath and a whisky and soda.

He sighed. He spent too much time thinking about the past. The present was difficult enough. He was lost and would stay lost unless he worked out where he was.

Freddie was due to meet up with his two oldest friends in the small town of Quillan at six o'clock that evening. Their idea was to have a few days walking in the mountains on the French-Spanish border. It was something of an annual tradition. They had met at boarding school, then gone to the same university. After three years of drinking and love affairs and study, they had gone their separate ways but stayed firm friends.

Each man found himself looking for work in the grim years after the end of the First World War. Brown did something in the City and was doing rather well. Turner had taken over the family boat-making business. Freddie had followed in his father's footsteps and become a teacher. He didn't enjoy it. He found the boys troublesome and the work dull. But there was nothing he would rather be doing. George's death had knocked the stuffing out of him. Since then, nothing seemed to matter much.

Brown and Turner had set off

together the previous weekend. They took the night crossing from Portsmouth and spent ten days driving down the west coast of France. Freddie had the boys' end-of-term exam papers to mark, so had not been able to get away.

He peered up through the windscreen. It looked like the weather was going to turn. The sky was grey, the colour of slate, and black clouds threatened rain. He glanced at the clock on the walnut dashboard of his little Ford. It was already two o'clock. There was no chance he'd make it by six.

Freddie studied the map for a few minutes more. There were only two options. He could press on or he could turn round and head back towards the last village. He thought that was where he had taken a wrong turning. But that was at least an hour ago. He couldn't afford to lose any more time.

Freddie shut the map book. He

put his driving cap and leather gloves back on and eased the little car into gear. If he was right, this road should meet up again with the main highway beyond this ridge.

He fixed his eyes on the road and carried on.

Chapter Two

Freddie heard a rumble of thunder in the distance. It echoed in the valley between the mountains. Then, a second growl of thunder sounded. Without further warning, a single fork of lightning split the grey sky.

Freddie felt a violent gust of wind hit the car. Then a single large drop of rain fell, the size of a penny, then another and another, faster, faster. Within seconds, the rain was drumming on the roof of the car. It bounced off the bonnet and splattered against the windows. Freddie turned the wipers on. Back and forward, back and forward, they made no difference.

There was more thunder. A second snap of lightning lit the entire sky. Freddie slowed right down, gripping the wheel tighter. He could see no more than a few feet ahead.

The tyres struggled to keep their hold on the slippery, steep road.

The sky was suddenly dark, black and threatening. Freddie turned on his headlights. Now the car was misting up. He wound down the window a little and felt a blast of cold, wet air. It made little difference. He leaned forward and wiped the inside of the windscreen with his sleeve. All the while, the sound of the wipers echoed in his head, back and forth, back and forth.

The crash of thunder came, the sound roaring through the valley. Then, a flash of lightning struck the road right ahead. Freddie slammed on the brakes, pulse jumping, heart thumping.

He counted, trying to work out how far away the storm was.

One, two, three . . . Seven seconds between the thunder and the lightning.

So the storm was still seven, maybe eight, miles away.

Freddie hit the accelerator pedal. He felt exposed out on this mountain road. He needed to find shelter.

The little car lurched forward into the raging head wind. Freddie told himself he wasn't really in any danger. The storm sounded worse than it was. The chances of the car being struck by lightning were small. Surely? There were too many tall trees around.

But he didn't convince himself. Besides, Freddie knew the real danger was the rain not the storm itself. If it kept up like this the road would become impassable. Already, rain was racing down the mountainside like a waterfall, cutting across the switchback bends in the road. Everywhere, there was swirling black floodwater.

There was another fierce crack of thunder directly overhead and a snap of lightning, sharp as a whip. Freddie braked and, to his horror, felt the car slide. He fought to keep on course.

He dragged down hard on the wheel, but too hard. It was too much, too late. The car skidded, gliding sideways across the road, towards the sheer drop on the left hand side. He shouted. Then, there was a sharp crack. The offside wing caught on a border of stones marking the tree line at the edge of the road. Desperate, Freddie pulled at the wheel the opposite way. There was nothing he could do. He was going to crash.

The car twisted round 180 degrees, spinning like a child's top.

Instinct took over. Freddie threw up his hands to protect his face. He felt the engine cut out, then a thud. Glass shattered into his lap. This was it. Any second now he would feel nothing but air beneath him as the car went over into the abyss.

He thought of his parents, his gentle mother and his stern father. How would they cope with the death of another son? He thought of his brother. Had George seen death coming to meet him? Did he know, in that last split second before the bullet found him, that his time was up?

Then the present rushed back. Freddie was thrown back in his seat. He heard a crack of metal and the car hit something. Freddie's head jerked forward and hit the dashboard. Pain, sharp and complete.

After that, he felt nothing.

Chapter Three

Freddie was out cold. It felt like hours, but was probably only minutes. Then he felt a tingling in his toes, his fingers. He was aware that his whole body hurt.

For a moment, he thought he was dreaming. Then, in a rush, it came back to him—the storm, the car hurtling across the road, the crash. He opened his eyes. His head was thumping loudly enough to wake the dead. The world came back into focus.

Freddie laughed out loud first with relief and then the luck of his narrow escape. The car was balanced on the edge of the cliff. The nearside wheels were over the edge, but the body of the car was still on the road.

He was facing the opposite way down the hill, but he was all right. He was alive.

Bit by bit, he worked out what had happened. The car had skidded, spun around and run into the marker stones at the side of the road. It was the trees, though, that stopped him heading straight over the edge.

Freddie let his head fall back against the seat. His heart was thudding like a drum. He could feel shards of glass in his lap. The thought of how close he had come gave him a sick, cold feeling in the pit of his stomach. He wiped his face. When he looked down, there was red blood, bright red, on the tips of his brown leather gloves.

The minutes passed. Still Freddie could not move. His legs had turned to jelly and his pulse was jumping still. The wind whistled around the car. The rain was still hammering down on the roof. He was soaking wet. But he was safe.

The moment of relief passed. Freddie knew he had to find help. Slowly, carefully, he reached out and opened the door. A violent gust of wind set the door flying back against the side. The car tipped dangerously.

Very slowly, Freddie put out first one leg, then the other. The wind was threatening to knock him off balance and made his ears ring. Inch by inch, he eased himself out of the car and managed to stand up.

Freddie closed the door, stepped back, then looked at the damage. The good news was that the body of the car was still on the road. Only the nearside wheels were overhanging the ravine. The bad news was that the front axle looked broken and the windscreen was gone. One thing was certain, he could not get the car back on the road on his own.

Freddie wasn't sure he could risk getting his overnight pack from the boot. He might send the car right over. He carefully opened his door and reached across to take the map book from the seat. Fighting to hold the pages steady in the wind, he saw there was a small village marked lower down the mountain, slightly off the main track.

Freddie locked the car. He put the keys in his pocket then headed back down the road to where a footpath was marked on the map.

Head down, collar pulled up, Freddie trudged down the hill. The wind boxed his ears. The rain drove into the back of his neck, his back, his knees. His tweed trousers were soaking wet and flapped against his legs. The world seemed to have turned to water. Everything shimmered silver, with not a dry patch of land or tree in sight. Although the wind was easing a little and Freddie had not heard thunder for some minutes, the rain was still falling, fast and furious. It bounced over the surface of the road like sparks from a firework.

Freddie sighed. His troubles were far from over. But, the truth was, he was glad to be alive.

Chapter Four

Apart from the odd trail of smoke from the valley below, there were no signs of human life at all. Nothing but trees and rocks and the sound of the rain.

After a while, Freddie found the path that appeared to lead off down through the woods. It was steep and overgrown, but wide enough for two people to walk side by side.

The rain was still falling but the branches of the trees gave him some shelter. As he walked, he could make out ruts left by the wheels of a cart and the hooves of a donkey or maybe an ox. His spirits lifted a little more. At least someone had passed this way before.

Soon, he found himself standing at the crossroads of two paths. To the left, there was a feeling of neglect

25

and stillness. The trees and evergreen bushes dripped with rain. Everything smelled sodden, wet. Oak leaves lay on the ground. The sharp needles of the fir trees bowed low over it.

The right-hand path was much steeper, but more direct. It plunged straight down the mountainside rather than running in a zigzag.

Freddie looked down at his leather shoes. The tips were stained dark and water was seeping in through the soles. He thought of his sturdy hiking boots left in his little car, then sighed. There was nothing to be done.

He took the right hand path. It had a lonely feel to it. There were no fresh wheel tracks. There was no sign that the leaves on the ground had been disturbed, no sense that anyone had recently passed this way. Even the air seemed colder. The going got rougher. Stones, uneven earth and fallen branches tumbled from the overgrown bushes on either side.

Freddie felt as if the mountain was closing in upon him. Shock had set in and his relief had faded. Now, the woods seemed strangely silent. No birds sang, no rabbits or foxes or mice moved in the undergrowth.

'A place of ghosts,' he muttered.

An April mist was now setting in, creeping up without warning. Freddie sped up. He started to imagine shapes, outlines, behind every tree. Once or twice he even turned round, sure that someone or something was watching him from the dark forest around him.

There was nothing there. No one.

Finally, the land levelled out. Freddie found himself standing on a patch of flat ground that looked down over a picture-postcard village. His eye was caught by a twist of grey smoke. He narrowed his gaze and looked more closely. Houses, dwellings, fires burning. Freddie gave a sigh of relief. He had made it.

Now he could pick out a cluster of red-tiled roofs, half shrouded in the mist. Freddie was cold and hungry and his legs felt as if they might give way under him at any moment. But now he was almost there, he felt a burst of energy and picked up his pace. In his mind he could already hear the comforting clatter of the cafés and bars, the rattling of plates in the kitchens, the sound of human voices.

Freddie walked fast across the wet ground towards a small stone bridge in the far corner of the field. As he crossed over, Freddie glanced down to the stream below. The water was racing, lapping against the underside of the bridge and splashing up over the banks.

Then, in the distance, Freddie heard the thin tolling of a church bell. The mournful single note was carried on the wind to where he stood listening. He counted the chimes.

He raised his eyebrows. Four o'clock. The last he remembered, the clock on the dashboard of the car was at two. Freddie listened until the last echo of the bell had died away then carried on across a second field covered with tiny blue and pink mountain flowers, like confetti scattered in a churchyard after a wedding. Around the edge of the field, poppies grew tall and bright red, like splashes of blood.

At last, Freddie reached the outskirts of the village. A white mist hung like a veil over everything, skimming the tops of the houses and buildings. The grass under his feet gave way to a track wide enough for a cart to pass along. The surface was muddy after the rain, the colour of gingerbread.

He came to a small wooden sign set at the side of the road.

He read the name of the village out loud. 'Larzat.'

Chapter Five

Freddie walked slowly into the village. He passed a few low buildings that looked like stores or animal pens. Then, as he got closer to the centre, the houses began.

Even allowing for the storm, the village seemed oddly empty. Nothing seemed to be open. Once he thought he heard footsteps in the distance, muffled by the mist. Once he thought he heard the bleating of sheep. But when he listened again, all was quiet.

The state of the road got better, the buildings more grand, the further he went. The larger houses had laurel trees in wide wooden planters outside their doors. But, still, he saw no one. No signs of day-to-day life. All the shops were boarded up and the wooden shutters firmly bolted.

Heavy, metal-framed gas lamps were set into the walls. The flames cast a weak yellow glow. But although the mist had lifted a little, there was something about the dusk, the stillness and the lack of life that made Freddie feel as if he had stepped into an old-fashioned photograph. He half expected to see gentlemen in old-fashioned coats and top hats walking past. Or nursemaids pushing babies in prams. Or little girls with their hair in ribbons and boys in sailor suits playing with wooden spinning tops.

Without warning, a memory of a family photograph came into his mind. It was the last one taken of them all together. His mother was seated, her long skirts spread out around her. He, a boy of ten, stood next to her. Their father, smart in his wing collar and black moustache, stood behind her with his hand on her shoulder. George, fine in his uniform, stood on the other side of his mother.

They were all smiling.

Freddie took a deep breath. George. It was more than ten years since his brother had gone missing. Freddie's dreams were still haunted by him, but he thought of George less often as the years went by. It was odd his brother was so much on his mind this afternoon.

'A place of ghosts,' he said again under his breath.

Freddie arrived at the small square in the centre of the village. It was bordered on three sides by buildings and lined by trees with silver bark. In the centre there was a stone well with high sides and, in one corner, a water trough for animals. Beside it he saw a small café with a yellow and white striped awning. It, too, was shut, the chairs were tipped forward against the round metal tables. A small church occupied most of the southern side of the square, with a single bell set high in the wall.

As his gaze moved around the square, Freddie found what he was looking for: a modest guest house, plain but respectable-looking. He walked over and up the three stone steps leading to a wide wooden door. A board above the door gave the names of the owners, Mr and Mrs Galy. Another sign stuck in the window, this one handwritten, said there were vacancies.

A brass bell hung on the wall. Freddie raised his hand to pull the rope when, suddenly, something made him pause. He had a prickling feeling on the back of his neck. He felt as if hidden eyes were watching him from behind the shutters and windows, the same feeling he'd had in the woods.

Freddie glanced behind him. Again, there was no one there.

'Pull yourself together,' he said to himself.

Freddie took off his hat, straightened his jacket, then rang the bell. At once, he heard footsteps behind the door. Moments later, it was opened by an old man in a flat-collared shirt, a waistcoat and heavy brown country trousers. His face was weather-beaten, lined by the years. White hair framed his face. Freddie guessed he must be Mr Galy, the owner.

'Yes?'

In halting French, Freddie asked if there was a room available for the night and tried to explain about the accident. Mr Galy at first said nothing, then shouted down the corridor. A stout, middle-aged woman dressed in black from head to toe appeared. Her heels clicked on the tiled floor as she came towards them.

Mrs Galy spoke some English, at least enough for Freddie to be able to explain how his car was stranded in the mountains above the village. She nodded. Then after a rattling conversation with her husband, too fast for Freddie to follow, said there was a local mechanic who could help.

'Tomorrow,' she said.

'Not this afternoon?'

Mrs Galy shook her head. 'It's too late. It will be dark soon. Tomorrow.'

Freddie shivered, suddenly aware of how cold he was. The cut on his forehead had started to ache. He felt very tired, bone-weary.

'That's fine,' he said. 'Tomorrow will be fine.'

Chapter Six

Freddie followed Mrs Galy down the long and narrow corridor.

Candles set in black iron holders on the walls flickered as they passed. The movement sent strange shadows dancing up to the ceiling. It was very quiet for a boarding house. There was no sound of conversation, not even any sound of the servants going about their duties.

'Are there other guests?' he asked.

Mrs Galy appeared not to hear him.

She stopped in front of a high wooden desk at the foot of the stairs. Freddie could smell the beeswax polish. The wood gleamed in the light from an oil lamp that sat on the counter top. She took a large, brass key from the row of hooks on the wall.

'This way,' she said.

Freddie followed her up the tiled staircase to a room on the second floor. Mrs Galy turned the key in the lock, pushed open the door and stood back for Freddie to walk in first.

He glanced around. It was plain, but pleasant and clean. Two tall windows, floor to ceiling, filled one side of the room. An old-fashioned bed with a brass bedstead stood against the left-hand wall. Beside it was a wooden bedside table. On the opposite side of the room, a gilt-framed mirror hung on the wall above a heavy chest of drawers. On the top sat a large white china bowl and matching jug.

'I could do with a bath,' he said, 'if that's not too much trouble. To warm up.'

Mrs Galy nodded. 'At the end of the landing,' she said. 'I will send up the maid with hot water and something for your head, yes?'

'My head?'

'You are hurt,' she said, pointing to the mirror. 'See?'

Freddie peered into the looking-glass and saw the trickles of dry blood and the patchwork of tiny cuts. He had not realised quite what a sight he looked.

'I hit my head when the car crashed,' he said.

Mrs Galy made to leave.

'Actually, there is one more thing,' Freddie added. 'I need to send word to my friends. They are in Quillan. I was due to meet them tonight. Is there a telegraph office? Or do you have a telephone, perhaps?'

'In the next town, yes. Not here.'

Freddie's heart sank.

'But if you care to write a message,' she said, pointing at the desk in the corner of the room, 'I will send a boy in the morning.'

'Thank you.'

Mrs Galy nodded. 'If you leave your clothes outside the door, I will see they are washed and dried for the morning. I will find something of my husband's for you to wear.'

Freddie smiled his thanks. 'That is most kind.'

Mrs Galy placed the key on the table. 'The dining room is at the foot of the stairs to the right. Dinner is served at six o'clock.'

Freddie stood still, listening to the sound of her shoes getting fainter and fainter in the corridor. Then he crossed to the desk. He wrote a brief message for his friends, put the note in an envelope, wrote the address of the boarding house where they were staying and sealed it.

That done, Freddie stripped off to his undergarments. He took the clean towel from the end of the bed and went in search of the bath.

Chapter Seven

As the clock struck six o'clock, Freddie locked his door, put the key in his pocket and went down to dinner. He felt much better. The cuts on his head were not as bad as he had feared and the borrowed clothes were a good fit.

Freddie left the letter for his friends on the counter top, then went to the dining room. He paused in the doorway for a moment and looked around. It was a good-sized room. A heavy oak sideboard filled one wall. Like his bedroom upstairs, there were two tall windows overlooking the square. The glass was covered by heavy velvet curtains that hung on gold rings. There were three sturdy square tables in the dining room, each laid for four. Each was set with white tablecloths, a knife, fork and spoon at each place, and a glass.

Several pairs of eyes turned to look at him. At one table sat two middle-aged women. They looked like one another and Freddie guessed they were sisters. They were talking in low voices and looking at a guidebook. Three men were sitting at the table in the middle of the room. At the table in the far corner, a young couple were gazing at one another. The tips of their fingers were touching.

Freddie gave a general nod of greeting. He did not fancy playing gooseberry. Nor did he want to get into conversation with the sisters, who looked a little severe. He headed for the men's table.

'May I join you?'

They introduced themselves, speaking in English, although Freddie found it hard to place their accent.

The meal passed pleasantly in light conversation, advice about the best walks in the region and talk of the bad weather. The maid arrived with jugs of water for each table, local red wine and a basket of bread. The meal was plain, but good—hard-boiled eggs, a plate of cold meats, salt pork, white goat's cheese and slices of chicken pie. For dessert, there was a bowl of a sugary white pudding rather like English custard.

After dinner was over, the sisters excused themselves. The young couple left shortly after, giggling and holding hands. Freddie and the three men remained for a while in the dining room, smoking. Mr Galy had no whisky, so they all tried a strong local spirit rather like brandy while the maid cleared up around them.

When she began to carry in breakfast things for the morning, Freddie and his companions knew they had outstayed their welcome and got up to leave.

The others decided to go to bed. Freddie, however, was wide awake. He kept reliving his day in his mind.

He knew he would not be able to go to sleep.

Freddie found Mr Galy and asked him to leave the bottle. He was getting rather a taste for the local brandy. By means of hand gestures, nods and winks, it was agreed he would pay in the morning.

With his round-bellied glass in one hand and the bottle in the other, Freddie crossed the hall and went towards the small parlour. The tall, long-case clock in the hall struck the hour. A little drunk, Freddie stopped and stared at the hands. The numbers on the clock face seemed to dance before his eyes. It was early still. Only nine o'clock.

Freddie raised his eyebrows. He supposed they kept early hours in the mountains. He would have a nightcap, perhaps smoke another cigarette. Then he would go up to bed.

The door to the parlour was closed. Freddie opened it gently, so as not to disturb anyone. The room was empty but a welcoming fire roared in the grate. There was a smell of resin, the scent of the forest, as the flames crackled and burned the logs.

There was a card table in the corner. He crossed the room, unsteady on his feet, and sat down heavily in a chair. Two decks of cards were stacked on the table. One pack had blue and white backs, the other red.

Freddie played several hands of patience. But even though the cards were good, his mind kept wandering.

Two armchairs were set on either side of the fireplace. They looked inviting. Freddie gave up his cards and took the chair furthest from the door. He put the bottle and glass down on the table a little too hard. The sound split the silence of the room.

'Sssh,' Freddie whispered to nobody.

He picked up a newspaper, but the French was too hard for him so he quickly gave up. He felt content, a little sleepy. He was quite happy to sit and do nothing—to think a little, perhaps, and turn over the events of the day in his mind.

The clock on the mantelpiece struck the quarter.

Freddie glanced at its white face and brass hands. He should go to bed. But he could not summon up the energy to move. The fire was crackling, and he was warm and well fed. He felt his eyelids shutting. Just a few minutes more and he would go up.

Chapter Eight

Freddie jolted awake. His neck was stiff, his shoulders were stiff. His mouth felt woolly with sleep and brandy. He ran his tongue over his teeth and realised he was thirsty.

Slowly, Freddie became aware of the musty smell of the room. He could no longer hear the flames in the grate. There was a smell of ash, too, as if the fire had burned low.

He opened his eyes, wondering what the time was. Still groggy from sleep, he turned his head to look at the clock. For some reason, he could not see the hands. But out of the corner of his eye, he saw something else.

Someone else.

There was a young woman. She was sitting upright and very still, opposite him, looking into the fire. Her skin was as white as china.

Freddie sat up in his chair. The movement caught her attention. She turned her head towards him. Two brown eyes framed by long, black lashes stared straight at him. Freddie felt his heart lurch in his chest. Then, without speaking, she turned away and went back to looking into the flames in the grate.

Awkward, Freddie felt he should apologise for disturbing her.

'I'm so sorry. I must have fallen asleep. So rude of me.'

The girl gave no sign she had heard him.

'If you would prefer to be alone, then of course . . .'

She gave a tiny shake of her head.

'Well, if you are sure you don't mind . . .' He tailed off.

Freddie picked up the newspaper again. From behind it, he glanced at the girl from time to time. She was young, maybe eighteen or nineteen years old, and very slight. Her hair was loose and hung in brown curls down her back, not cut short in the modern style. In fact, there was something old-fashioned about her. She looked like a heroine in a Victorian poem. Her clothes were out of date. She wore a heavy red cloak over narrow shoulders, despite the heat of the room. Beneath the cloak, she seemed to be wearing a long dress. Fancy dress? He could see the green material beneath the hem of the cloak.

Freddie realised he was hot. He loosened the collar of his borrowed shirt. He could do with a glass of water. But he didn't want to leave the room to fetch one for fear the girl would vanish.

Who was she?

He took another gulp of brandy. Was she a guest? If she was, why had she not been at dinner? Or perhaps she was a daughter of the house? Miss Galy? He dismissed that idea too. If that were the case, she would be in the family room not sitting in the front parlour.

Freddie folded the newspaper. He felt fuddled and a little sick. The silence, the drink, falling asleep in the chair, all added up to a nagging headache.

The logs in the fire were spitting again. The clock was still ticking. The sounds were like the heartbeat of the room itself.

Since the girl was clearly not in the mood to talk, he knew he might as well go to bed. There was no point sitting here, in silence, just in case. He wondered why his nerves were sloshing around in his stomach. For some reason, he felt as if he was waiting for something to happen.

'Are you an honest man?'

Freddie was so deep in thought, the question made him jump.

'You have the look of an honest man.'

She spoke in English but in an accent Freddie had never heard before. Not quite French, not quite

Spanish, but something between the two. Her voice was deeper, less childlike than he expected.

'I . . . I suppose I am,' he managed to reply. 'Yes, I would say so.'

'And a man of courage?'

Her gaze was fierce, intense.

'Well, I would like to think so,' he said. 'If need be, then yes.'

Freddie felt like a butterfly pinned on a board.

'And a man who can tell true from false?'

'Certainly.'

She seemed to be weighing him up, judging him. Freddie realised he was holding his breath. Then she held out her hand, palm up. Freddie pulled his chair closer, so close their knees were almost touching.

'May I confide in you? Tell you a story?'

'Yes,' he said, too quickly. 'Yes, of course.'

Freddie realised he would have agreed to anything so long as she kept talking. 'Is it a true story?' he asked.

She tilted her head to one side. 'That is for you to judge.'

Freddie remembered his manners. He half stood up and held out his hand.

'I'm Frederick Smith. My friends call me Freddie.'

He waited for her to return the favour. She did not.

He hesitated again, awkward, then sat back down in his chair. All normal rules of behaviour seemed not to matter to her.

'I'm listening,' he said.

Chapter Nine

'I was born on an afternoon in spring,' she said. 'The world was coming back to life after a hard winter. The snow had melted. The streams were flowing again. Tiny mountain flowers of blue and pink and yellow filled the fields of the upper valley. My father said that on the day I was born he heard the first cuckoo sing. It was a good omen, he said.

'I was wrapped in linen cloth. Our neighbours came with a loaf they had baked. White flour, my father said, not the coarse brown grain used for every day. Others in the village also came with gifts: a brown woollen blanket for winter, a drinking cup, a wooden box with spices inside—and most precious, salt wrapped up in a piece of cotton dyed blue.

'It was May. The sheep were back

in the summer pastures. Every autumn, the shepherds took their flocks to Spain on the other side of the mountains. Each spring, when the air grew warm again, the men and the animals returned.'

As she talked, Freddie noticed she looked happy. Then, like a cloud crossing the face of the sun, her face grew serious.

'I was the first child to be born in our village since . . . since the troubles began.'

The word brought back a memory. Freddie thought of the last time George came home on leave. He, too had talked of the 'troubles', of how rumour had it the Germans were turning their guns on civilians, attacking villages for the sport of it. Not soldiers, but women and children. George had not spelled things out in full. He had not needed to.

Freddie braced himself for what might be coming.

'My mother and father were well liked,' she carried on quietly. 'My father wrote letters for those in our village who could not read or write. He helped the priest give advice to those who were accused of crimes. He cared for the weak and those in need. He himself was not a man of strong faith, but he was a good man.'

Freddie nodded.

'At first, the troubles did not affect our village so much. The struggle had been going on for some years— many years, indeed. What fighting there was happened far away. We thought that our village was safe in the folds of the mountains, this far from the heart of things.'

'I say, don't upset yourself,' Freddie said quickly. 'There's no need to go on if it is too difficult.'

'There is every need,' she said. 'When it is a matter of truth.'

She paused. When she spoke again, her voice was clearer, sharper.

'How much do you know of our

54

history, Mr Smith, about the land, the traditions, our way of life in our part of France?'

Freddie was surprised by the sudden change of subject, but managed to reply. 'Only the usual, I suppose. The sort of stuff one reads in a guidebook. Pretty basic.'

She nodded. 'For years and years, we lived under the threat of attack. We feared the enemy soldiers, the courts, the spies, their prisons. Our beliefs and theirs did not agree. We lived always waiting for the blow to fall. Not able to trust anyone.'

'You trusted me,' he said.

She gave a sad smile. 'Things are different.'

'I suppose they are.'

Freddie was turning things over in his head. He didn't think the Germans had got this far south. He thought all the fighting had been in the trenches of northern France, and in Belgium. But, then, he did not know much. He had been a child.

'For years, we thought we had been forgotten. But, finally, it happened. They came for us.'

Chapter Ten

Freddie realised he was holding the arms of the chair. When he glanced down, he saw his knuckles were white.

He took a deep breath. However grim, whatever she was about to tell him, it was long over now. The horror belonged in the past.

'Go on,' he said, but steeling himself.

'It was a beautiful day. Later, I remember thinking how wrong it was, that something so terrible should happen on a morning of such light, such blue skies.

'My family was lucky. We were visiting friends on the other side of the mountains. We had set off early, at dawn, to make our way back to the village. The mist still hung low in the valley. The sun was not yet high in the sky. On the outskirts, where the woods come down right to the village, we saw a boy, a friend of my brother, running. He said soldiers had been seen, a thin line of men making their steady way towards us. He said . . .'

Freddie could not help himself. 'What? What did he say?'

'That they were burning the villages of the lower valley,' she said. 'He said men, women and children had been cut down where they stood.

'Without delay, we hurried to the square. All was uproar. People were crying, shouting. Some wanted to stay, refusing to believe that the threat was real. Others wanted to defend our village against any attack. Others again, who had seen the terror, knew that to stay would be to sign your own death warrant.

'The Marty sisters said they were too old to be driven from their homes again. They refused to leave. A young couple, married but a week, had gone out early and had not returned. Some of the men chose to stay. To cause a diversion, if need be, to stop the soldiers from seeing our tracks into the mountains. Peter Galy, Michel Auty and his sons, William and Paul, also stayed.'

'I'm surprised there were so many men left,' Freddie said. 'Hadn't all the men of fighting age been called up?'

'It was different here.'

He had a prickling feeling at the base of his spine. He couldn't put his finger on it, but what she said didn't make sense. He had passed monuments to the dead in every village, every town. In the graveyards of every church, there were lists of the fallen—fathers, sons, friends, brothers. All the men had gone.

But before he could ask her another question, she was talking again.

'There was only enough time to gather what we could carry on our backs and leave. A loaf of bread, wine, blankets for the cold mountain nights, my father's ink and paper.

As the sun rose in the sky, my parents, my brother and I joined those heading up into the woods. My brother was ten then. He was a weak boy, thin and often ill, but so strong in spirit. Brave.

'We travelled by foot. We could not risk taking the animals, the cart, for fear the tracks would give us away. The mules, the sheep, the goats, these too we left behind. We dared to hope they would be there when we returned.'

Freddie frowned. 'But where did you go? There must have been so many of you.'

She looked at him for a moment, as if surprised he needed to ask such a question.

'There are caves within these mountains, hidden from view.'

'Enough to provide shelter for an entire village?'

She nodded. 'Some caves are small

and linked by narrow tunnels. In other places, there are underground cities within the mountains—tunnels, caves, hidden places. Each family found somewhere to rest.' She paused. 'Besides, we did not think we would be there long.'

Questions were nagging at Freddie. So many things did not add up or fit with what he knew.

'But if you knew where the caves were, how did the soldiers not hear of them? Someone must have talked? Someone always does.'

She shook her head. 'They had not been used for many years before that.'

He frowned again thinking how odd it was she gave the impression of so much time passing. The war had begun in 1914 and run its grim course until 1918. They were terrible years certainly, but only four years in all.

Her voice cut in to his thought. 'The soldiers knew we could not have gone far. They searched and searched. The cave in which we found shelter was some way up the highest peak. Ancient roots from the old trees formed steps in the ground. The only way in or out was a small opening in the mountain. From below, it looked like a half moon cut into the rock face, just a semicircle of stone. It did not appear to lead anywhere and seemed like a dead-end.'

'So you lived there for days? Weeks?'

'Longer than that. Spring tipped into summer. Later, the leaves turned gold on the trees. Still they did not find us. Later, the snows came. We thought they would leave, but they did not. They kept watch.'

'Your brother,' he said. 'How did he cope with the winter?'

'He did not,' she said quietly. 'The cold was in his bones, in his chest. He needed fresh air and sunlight and good food, the very things we could not give him.' Her voice dropped to a whisper. 'He never complained. Even when he was suffering, he bore it bravely.'

Grief turned her brown eyes to black.

'I could not save him,' she said.

Chapter Eleven

'I'm so sorry,' he said.

Freddie knew how grief could creep up at any moment. He knew how the pain was as sharp as a needle under the skin. Then how, even as time went by, it became a dull ache, it was always there, always tugging at the corner of things. A familiar friend.

'I could not save him,' she said again.

He understood how that played upon her mind. In the first months after George had been reported missing, the thought of his body lying unclaimed on the battlefield haunted him more than anything.

Freddie never talked about George's death. He didn't admit to anyone how deeply he mourned his brother still.

But, for the first time in more than

a decade, Freddie wanted to speak. Needed to speak.

'I, too, lost a brother,' he said.

This time, it was she who reached across the space between them. She took his hand. Her touch was so light, Freddie could hardly feel it. Her skin was like tissue paper. The cloak slipped from her shoulders and he saw clearly she was wearing a long green dress with an old-fashioned belt. Attached to it was a leather pouch, like a purse or small bag. Such strange, out-of-date clothes.

Freddie began to talk, slowly at first, then faster. Ten years and more of grief, of loss, of silence, came tumbling out. In the room, the fire crackled. Time seemed to stand still as he talked and talked.

At last, there was nothing left to say. All emotion was spent. His head was empty. Freddie took a deep breath.

'I'm sorry, I . . . I don't know what came over me.'

65

He felt, for a fleeting moment, the pressure of her fingers on the palm of his hand. Then, slowly, she withdrew.

He was tired now, so tired. But he felt as if a weight had been taken from his shoulders.

'All I meant to say, before . . . well. I was supposed to comfort you, not the other way around. I only wanted to let you know that I understood.'

'I knew you were haunted already,' she said softly. 'How else could I speak to you?'

Freddie wasn't sure what she meant. 'So,' he said, eager to make amends for his loss of control. 'You saw out the winter. And, when it was over? You came back?'

The look on her face stopped him. It struck him that he had disappointed her.

'No one came back. Not one.'

Freddie realised he had missed something. He knew she had lost her brother, but what of her parents?

66

She, herself, was here after all.

'I don't understand,' he said. 'Some of you must have come back.'

He saw her fists were clenched in her lap. He noticed how long her fingers were and how her nails were pale, not painted red like the modern fashion.

'The soldiers were just waiting out the winter. When the thaw began, just when we dared to think we were safe, they moved against us.'

Freddie still didn't understand. He shook his head. The movement made his head spin. The whole room seemed to lurch. He suddenly realised he was more drunk than he had thought.

'But here you are,' he said. Even to his ears, the words sounded odd, as if he was speaking under water.

Now Freddie was struggling to keep his head. There seemed to be two girls now, both looking at him with their brown eyes. He needed a glass of water, or a strong coffee.

He tried to stand up, but his legs didn't obey him.

'You should rest,' she said gently. Her voice seemed to come from a long way away.

Freddie could not keep his eyes open any longer. The warmth of the room, the gentle rise and fall of her voice, were washing over him. He felt his arms grow heavy, his shoulders, his neck, his legs.

'You never did tell me your name.'

He seemed to hear her speak deep inside his head. A single word, whispered in his mind.

'Marie,' she whispered. 'My name is Marie.'

He was so tired, so very tired. 'A few minutes and I'll be as right as rain.'

Freddie felt his eyes close. He sensed a movement, a subtle shifting of the air. Then she spoke again.

'Find us,' she said. 'Find us and bring us home.'

They were the last words Freddie heard her say.

Chapter Twelve

'Mr Smith?'

Freddie heard his name. He felt a hand on his shoulder, shaking him awake. Slowly, he pulled himself back from sleep. His whole body ached and his head was thudding.

'Sir? Mr Smith?'

He recognised the voice of Mrs Galy. Freddie opened his eyes. He took in the room, cold and empty in the grey morning light. The fire had burned out in the grate.

He saw the brandy bottle and glass, both empty, on the table by his chair.

Then he remembered how the night had passed. Talking, remembering, thinking of the past. He sat up straight, and stared at the chair where Marie had been sitting.

It was empty.

'Are you unwell?'

Freddie cast his eyes around the room again. He saw nothing, no sign of her.

'No, no, I'm fine. Forgive me. I was talking to another guest last evening. I must have drifted off to sleep here. She was a young woman, with long brown hair. I wonder if you have seen her this morning?'

Mrs Galy shook her head.

'She was wearing rather old-fashioned clothes, I suppose,' he said. 'A long red cloak and a green dress.'

Freddie lifted his hands and rubbed his sore temples. He could feel the after-effects of the brandy.

'I came in here to play a hand of cards, read the newspaper. I dropped off. When I woke, she was here. She said her name was Marie,' he added, his voice rising.

Mrs Galy looked confused, worried even. 'We have no guest of that name, sir.'

'What about among the kitchen

staff? Or someone from the village?'

Mrs Galy shook her head. 'Not that I can think of, sir. I'm sorry.'

'You're sure?'

It came to him that Marie might have been here without Mrs Galy knowing. It had been late, after all.

Freddie glanced at the clock, the hands now clear. To his surprise, it was six forty-five in the morning. He stood up. He was clearly not going to get anywhere with Mrs Galy. He would ask about Marie in the village instead. Perhaps one of the maids would know who she was.

'Tell me, Mrs Galy, was there much enemy action here during the war?'

Her face showed her surprise at this question. But she answered.

'Not really, sir. There was a camp not so far from here for prisoners of war, though it is a good many hours' drive away.'

Freddie frowned. 'What about German units operating in the area?'

Mrs Galy shook her head. 'Things were not easy, but we were better off than many. The village lost men fighting on the northern front.'

Her eyes darted to the clock. She clearly wanted to get on with her work. But Freddie couldn't let it drop.

'So this village was never invaded? Or attacked in any way?'

'No, sir.'

Freddie didn't understand.

'If there is nothing else, I need to prepare the breakfast. I have asked Michel Auty, who works in the garage, to be here at eight o'clock. You can show him to your car.'

Freddie hardly heard. Thoughts were spinning around in his head, like leaves blown by the wind. He racked his brains. He realised that Marie had never actually said she was talking about the recent war. But given her age, it was a reasonable guess. Now he came to think about it, she had never actually said that she came from here. But again, it was a reasonable guess. Her descriptions of the flight from the village, the journey into the mountains and the cave had been so clear.

'Mr Smith? Will eight o'clock suit you? For the car?' she said slowly, as if talking to a child.

Freddie forced his attention back to the matter in hand. 'Yes, sorry. Quite. That will do very well, thank you.'

Mrs Galy picked up his empty glass and bottle and plumped the cushion in the chair. She cast an expert eye around the room, checking all was as it should be, then left.

Freddie did not move. The air settled around him. He heard Mrs Galy's footsteps getting fainter as she went down the corridor. He looked around the room once more. The newspaper was where he had left it. The two decks of cards were stacked on the table. Freddie glanced back to the chair where Marie had sat. The cushion was not even dented.

Had he been dreaming? He had fallen asleep in front of the fire. The day had been difficult and tiring, what with the accident, his head, the brandy, thoughts of George. He had drunk too much.

But even so.

On the mantelpiece, the little clock chimed the hour. The sound brought Freddie back to the present. He needed to wash and dress. He could do with a cup of strong coffee. Then, he had to think about sorting out the car with the mechanic.

He went into the corridor, still thinking about Marie. When he drew level with the desk at the foot of the stairs, Freddie noticed the guest register was open. He glanced around. There was no one about. Freddie turned the book to face him. Quickly, he scanned the names on the page. His own was the last entry in the book. Above his name were those of his dinner companions. Above them, in a woman's looping handwriting, were Mr and Mrs Perdu. The newlyweds, he supposed. Freddie turned back a page and ran his finger up the names from the bottom. As he had thought, the older ladies were sisters or, at least, shared a surname—Marty.

He frowned. There was something familiar about the name, although he could not place it. Now he came to think about it, all the names were somehow familiar.

The only one missing was Marie.

Chapter Thirteen

For the next few hours, Freddie did not have time to think about her.

Mr Auty arrived promptly at eight o'clock with his two sons. One of them, William, spoke good English so he translated between Freddie and his father. Freddie described his route and Mr Auty worked out where the car had crashed.

The air was fresh and sharp as the small group set off into the mountains. The sun had not yet cleared the top of the nearest hill. The early morning chill pinched at Freddie's cheeks but the bad weather of the previous day had gone. The sky was an endless blue, unbroken by clouds.

They left the village by the path Freddie had taken the afternoon before. As he looked around, it seemed as if spring had come overnight. The leaves on the oak and beech trees were coming into leaf. There was colour everywhere, in the meadows, in the woods up ahead, in the pale sun rising behind the mountain. He remembered Marie's description of the countryside. It was so precisely a mirror of what he saw. He was certain she had been talking about this valley, these mountains.

The four men crossed the bridge. Today the river was fast-flowing, but no longer threatening to burst its banks. Freddie saw the silver flash of fish in the stream. The green river weeds shimmered in the current, swaying this way and that. It was all so calm, so peaceful.

After a quarter of an hour, they reached the outskirts of the woods. Freddie pointed out the path he had followed. In single file, they left the brightness of the fields for the shade of the wood.

The path was steep and uneven. Yet it seemed an easier walk than yesterday, Freddie thought, even though they were walking uphill. The easy company of Michel and his two sons, the sun, the lack of wind and rain, all lifted his spirits. Today, Freddie no longer felt the presence of ghosts in the woods.

Before long, they arrived at the point where the footpath went up on to the road. Freddie pointed up the hill and they walked on in single file. In the trees, Freddie heard birdsong. There was a blackbird, a thrush, maybe even a robin. His brother had loved to be outside and knew the different calls of the birds. Freddie smiled. They seemed such English sounds to hear in a French country wood. A hawk wheeled overhead.

The sun was nearly up behind the mountain now. Its bright rays painted the surface of the leaves gold. After another five minutes, the rescue party reached the spot. To Freddie's relief, his Ford was just where he had left it. It had neither fallen over the cliff nor come loose from the tree. William took the coil of rope from his shoulder and fixed it around the front bumper. With his brother's help at the rear, they pulled. Slowly, the car was dragged back up on to the road, little by little.

The air was still cool, but it was hard work and the sun was hot for April. Michel, sweat glistening from his brow, looked the car over. With his drooping grey moustache and thick eyebrows, he looked more like an opera singer than a mechanic. But he seemed to know what he was doing.

He pointed at the axle, then at the front wheel arch, which had buckled. Next he kicked the side panel with the tip of his boot. With William's help translating, Freddie was left in no doubt that there was a fair amount of damage. It was going to be far from easy to fix. From the look on Michel's face, it looked as if the car was going to need quite a lot of work to get it back on the road. And, no doubt, it would cost. But they were talking too fast for him and their accents were strong.

While the men debated, Freddie settled himself on a boulder to wait. The sun, the smell of the pine trees, the gentle cry of the birds in the trees were all restful. He realised he felt calm. He felt more peaceful than he had for some time, in fact for as long as he could remember.

He found his mind straying to Marie. Freddie looked up at the great wall of rock ahead of him. Then he saw it. Slowly, he got to his feet and looked harder. Was it was just a trick of the light? He shielded his eyes. High up in the hills above him, he could just make out an opening in the rock. There seemed to be no way up. He tilted his head back to get a clearer view.

No, it was there. The mouth of a cave, carved into the mountainside. To the left, there was another opening, a little smaller, a little lower. Like two hollow eyes in a skull. A little further over, there was another cave.

At that moment, William put his hand on Freddie's shoulder. Freddie jumped.

'There is some damage to the chassis,' he said. 'My father can have it towed to the garage. Once he has examined it properly, he will have a better idea of how much work needs to be done.'

Freddie was not listening. 'Are those caves up in the mountain?' He pointed. 'There, just above that ridge?'

William followed the line of his finger, then nodded.

'Is it possible to get up there?' Freddie asked. 'From here, I mean.'

'You could climb up from the road, but it would be hard going. There is an easier path out of the village to that part of the mountain. Through the woods, not the fields.'

Freddie felt a memory slide across the surface of his mind. 'The woods?'

William nodded. 'The woods come down closer to the village at that point. It is a more sheltered route.' He looked at Freddie with his patient, unhurried face. 'So, shall we take the car back to the garage, or . . . ?'

Freddie was still looking up into the mountain. 'Yes. Yes, of course. Whatever your father advises, that is fine.'

William went to talk to Michel, who gave Freddie the thumbs-up sign and a wide smile. With Paul's help, Freddie got his bag out of the boot. He changed his shoes for his proper hiking boots. Then, with William carrying his case, they set off back to Larzat.

As they stepped off the main road, Freddie gave a last glance over his shoulder. He could no longer see the opening to the cave. But it was enough to know it was there. A plan was already forming in his mind. If, as he feared, his car would not be ready today, then he would climb up and explore.

If he could not find any trace of Marie in the village, then maybe he would have better luck finding the cave itself.

Chapter Fourteen

Michel did what he had promised and the car was quickly brought back to the village. After ten minutes of peering under the bonnet and up at the chassis, Michel told Freddie it would take at least two days to repair. Freddie stood about in the forecourt of the garage. Each time he asked how things were going, he was shooed away. He started to feel like an expectant father being chased from the delivery room by bossy nurses.

He decided to have an early lunch and then put into action his plan to search for the cave. He strolled into the square. Freddie noticed the tobacconist in the corner of the square was open. With the sound of the church bells at his back, ringing for midday, he got there just as the shopkeeper was closing.

The shop was long and narrow and cool inside. At the far end was a glass counter in front of a wall filled with different brands of cigarettes, tobaccos and cigars. On one side were glass display cases containing penknives and pipes. On the other was a shelf of newspapers and booklets of local interest. Most looked rather moth-eaten and yellow-edged and had clearly been there for some time.

Freddie scanned the row slowly reading the titles.

'English?' he asked.

The owner pointed to a small section at the back of the rack. Freddie chose a slim guidebook with a Union Jack printed in the top right-hand corner. He fished out a note from his wallet. As he took his change, Freddie asked the question he had been asking around the village all morning. Did the shopkeeper know a woman called Marie? Freddie got the same response as in the garage, the baker, the butcher and the general stores: a slow shake of the head and a no.

Another dead-end.

Freddie found a table outside the café in the sun. He ordered a ham omelette and a glass of red wine then sat back with the book. He opened it flat, cracking the spine. It was a simple text, printed in double columns on rough white paper. From the clumsy turns of phrase, he guessed it had been translated from French. Rather than a tourist guide, as he had thought, it turned out to be more of a history book. It told the story of a particular group of Christians who had lived in the region during the thirteenth and early fourteenth centuries. The Catholic Church had opposed them and they were forbidden to worship as they wished. Their property was taken away. Members of the group were tortured and condemned in unfair courts, imprisoned and executed. The last priest, said the book, had been burned at the stake in 1328. It was the end for the religion and its followers.

Then Freddie read something that made his heart lurch. According to the author, whole villages took refuge in caves. The evidence showed that the soldiers walled up many of the openings. Even as recently as the seventeenth century, caves were discovered containing countless bodies of those buried alive.

Freddie laid the book down on the table.

During the course of the morning, his belief in Marie had come and gone. Sometimes he was certain she had been there. They had talked all night, of war, of death, of the sadness they carried inside them. She had her ghosts, he had his. But then doubts crept in. No one had heard of her. No one had seen her.

Freddie looked down at the book.

Somehow, this changed things. Here was proof that local people had sought refuge in the caves six hundred years ago. And, if they had done so six hundred years ago, then why not ten years ago? As she had said.

Freddie drained his glass of red wine and called for the bill. There were three, maybe four, hours of daylight left. He intended to make good use of them.

Half an hour later, armed with a map, compass and his rucksack, Freddie set out again. He found the path William said led directly up into the heart of the mountains.

As he climbed, he tried to recall Marie's words about their journey and the landmarks they passed on the way. The summer pastures, the sun at their heels, the trees along their route. Most of all, he remembered the natural steps from the roots of an ancient tree that led up to the cave. She had not said so, but Freddie didn't think her family would have gone so far. They would have been keen to get out of sight as soon as possible. Besides, it would be hard going with an ill child.

Freddie didn't allow himself to question why he was doing what he was doing. Having decided on a course of action, he was determined to stick to it. He felt more alive than he had for some time, as if he finally had a purpose, an interest in life again.

Why Marie should have confided in him, a stranger, he did not know. Could her family still be lying up there in the caves? Surely she would have had their bodies brought down long ago?

Freddie kept going as the sun climbed higher in the sky. The shadows shortened.

Chapter Fifteen

After nearly an hour, he reached a flat open area, like a glade, ringed by trees. The rocks were covered with grass and moss. And hidden by the branches of the trees, he noticed, at last, an opening in the rock. Then he saw another.

Freddie sat on a rock and drank water from his flask. He waited until he got his energy back then went to explore. Here, at this level, there were some five or six openings. To his untrained eye, they all looked natural rather than man-made. But from here, he could see that some were large enough for two or three people to stand inside at the same time. Others were small and narrow. Others again were long and flat, only just big enough for a person to get inside on their hands and knees.

Freddie peered inside each then

moved on to the next. Some went back ten or twelve feet. Others led nowhere, no more than hollows in the rock.

The patterns on the rocks showed the passage of time. The wind and the rain had sculpted the stone over thousands of years. It reminded Freddie of pictures of tombs in the Holy Land. Here everything was green and grey and brown, rather than the yellow of the desert, but the beauty took his breath away.

He spread out the map and fixed his position with his finger. He realised he would need to climb higher to find the caves he had seen from the road. None of these caves matched the description of Marie's cave.

On the map, it looked as if there was another flat area a few hundred feet higher up. He checked the directions with his compass, then carried on further. The lack of sleep and the hard effort meant his legs felt like lead, but he did not give up.

Freddie glanced at the sky. It must be well after two o'clock. He was aware he must give himself enough time to get back to the village before darkness fell. He knew there were bears and wild cats in the mountains, perhaps even wolves.

He covered the distance quickly. At this next level, there were four caves. Each looked out over the valley below like dead eyes. The caves were reached by a narrow path that ran in front of the rock to the left-hand side. To the right was a sheer drop. The land fell away to nothing.

Freddie smiled. He was certain he had found the caves he had seen from the road earlier. Trying not to look down, he inched his way along the path. He leaned his shoulder against the rock to steady himself and tried not to think about what would happen if he fell.

But although each cave was large

enough to provide shelter, still none of them matched Marie's description. Then Freddie noticed a narrow path that ran up between two rocks. He looked at it more closely. With a jolt, he saw that the roots of trees had threaded themselves into a natural staircase.

Marie had talked of just such a thing. Freddie gave a sigh of relief. It was evidence he was on the right track at least. A few more steps, then he saw it. Right above his head was an opening the shape of a half moon. He scrambled up and clambered on to the ledge.

He had found it.

Chapter Sixteen

Freddie peered into the darkness of the cave.

At its highest point, the opening was about four feet high and five or six feet wide. The smell of wet, of earth, of the past was strong. Freddie turned over a rock with the tip of his boot. The damp soil was alive with worms and beetles exposed suddenly to the light.

Slowly, his eyes got used to the gloom. Velvet black gave way to grey. Freddie felt the short hairs rise on the back of his neck. He felt a sense of unease. He didn't believe in ghosts. And, after George's death, he had learned that real horror lay in the acts of men, not in childish fears of the dark. But now, standing in so lonely a place, Freddie felt a shudder go down his spine.

He took a deep breath, then

stepped inside.

Straight away, the smell of long-hidden, undisturbed air surrounded him. It was cool and damp. He rummaged in his rucksack for a torch. The beam was weak, but it lit the area just in front of him. It sent the shadows dancing up along the jagged grey walls of the cave.

Freddie walked slowly. He felt the ground sloping down beneath his feet, gritty and uneven. Loose stones and small pieces of rock crunched under his feet. He was aware of the daylight getting fainter at his back.

Then, without warning, the path came to an abrupt end. Freddie stopped dead. He could go no further. A wall of stone, of rock, of wood blocked his way. Freddie shone his torch to the roof to see if there had been a rock fall, but there were no signs of it. In which case, he reasoned, the stones must have been put here by human hands. He had a cold, hollow feeling in the pit of his stomach. Marie had said the soldiers did not find them and, yet, she had also said no one had come home. The book, however, had explained how, hundreds of years ago, the soldiers had walled up their victims inside the mountain. Could they have used the same trick in the last war?

With a sense of urgency, Freddie began to dig. He pulled at the stones, using both hands. He worked hard, stopping only to drink water from his flask. But, although the pile of rocks on his side got bigger, the wall did not seem smaller. Soon, his hands were scratched and bleeding. His arms ached and his knees hurt from kneeling on the hard ground. But he was driven by a wild need to know what lay behind the rocks.

At the back of his mind, Freddie did know why this mattered to him so much. He was doing for Marie and her family what he had not been able to do for his own. He should have brought George home to England and laid his body to rest in the earth. The dead should be remembered by a name on a tombstone. His brother deserved no less. Marie's brother and her parents deserved it too.

Finally, the wall began to give crumble. Freddie coughed and held his arm across his mouth as the dust filled the cave. Pieces of wood, stone and rock started to come loose. Within minutes, there was an opening as big as his hand. Freddie clawed at the gap until there was enough space for him to get through. He shone the torch into the darkness ahead, into the tomb.

Chapter Seventeen

On the far side of the wall, the air was colder.

Freddie put out his hand. Here the walls of the cave were damp to the touch. The surface beneath his feet was different too. It was no longer stone and gravel and dust, but smooth. It was slippery. More than once, he lost his footing and stumbled.

His unease grew with every step down into the endless darkness.

Finally, the tunnel came to an end. Freddie looked around him in awe. He was standing at the entrance to a huge cavern, like a cathedral hidden in the mountains. He shone his torch up and around in wonder.

'A city in the mountains,' he said.

That was how Marie had described their hiding place. Standing here, Freddie understood what she had meant. He took a step forward, then another. He no longer felt afraid. He no longer felt alone. He felt a sense of peace, quiet and calm. It was timeless, unchanging, far from the cares of the world.

Then, out of the corner of his eye, he saw something strange. Not rock or stone, but something man-made. Was it a pile of clothes or belongings? Freddie caught his breath. A grave? This was what he had come to find. But his legs were trembling and the beam of light jumped in his hands.

Freddie walked closer. Now, there was no doubt. People, lying side by side. From this distance they looked as if they were sleeping. He walked nearer, closer. His heart lurched. He could see clothes, material, heavy cloth.

The sound caught in his throat. Not people, skeletons. Bones. Dead sockets where once had been eyes. The skulls were a green-white in the pale beam of the torch. He felt his stomach lurch. He swallowed deeply and dug in his pocket for a handkerchief to hold over his nose and mouth.

As Freddie struggled to keep his nerve, he tried to work out what he was looking at. If he had found Marie's family, how could their bodies have rotted so completely in so short a period of time? Even if they had died at the beginning of the war, in 1914, rather than at the end, would there not be some flesh left on the bones? In such conditions, away from the light and the wet and fresh air, surely the bones would not yet be picked clean by time?

He swept his gaze over the makeshift grave. He saw fragments of cloth, a clay bowl, the stump of a candle. These were the humble objects that the family had treasured as they waited to die. They were side by side, as if they had simply lain down together and gone to sleep.

Freddie stepped carefully between the bodies. There were two larger skeletons, then one much smaller. He assumed this was Marie's brother.

Then a fourth.

Freddie's legs started to shake. Marie said her mother and father and brother had taken refuge in the cave. She had not said anyone else was with them.

Now he noticed a sheet of paper on the ground. He took his handkerchief away from his face and held it in his fingers. Then he bent down and gently pulled the paper free. It was brittle to the touch, more like parchment than normal paper. Beneath, he could see there were many more sheets, scattered around the bones like fallen leaves in autumn.

Careful not to disturb things more than he had to, Freddie gathered up the individual sheets. The handwriting was the same on each, scratchy, uneven and black on the yellow surface. He did not recognise the language. Some words looked like French, others more like Spanish.

At last, only one sheet remained. It was held between the white skeletal fingers, as if the author was still writing when their final breath left them.

Freddie skimmed it with his eyes.

'When all else is done, only words remain.'

His eyes jumped to the bottom of the sheet. There was a date. His stomach lurched. April 1328.

How could that be? If this was Marie's family, and all the signs were that it was, then the date was six hundred years too early.

His thoughts slipped back to the history book he had bought and read in the café, about the wars of the fourteenth century. Freddie shook his head. How could he explain how he, a stranger to the region, have stumbled on a grave dating back to the Middle Ages? It would have been found long before now.

Then again, if he had not known where to look, he would have assumed there was nothing there. A solid wall of stone and rock barred the way. It looked like a dead-end. It was possible.

Freddie glanced back down at the name at the bottom of the antique paper. What he read next knocked the breath out of him. He shook his head in disbelief.

How could he explain this? He didn't want to explain it. Now he noticed, for the first time, what lay around the skeleton. The bones were wrapped in a red cloak, grown ragged at the edges. Beneath, there were glimpses of a heavy green dress. He looked and saw the brown leather pouch, like a purse, attached to a belt.

Freddie's head was spinning. The air in the cave seemed suddenly stale, old. He felt it in his mouth, his lungs, choking him. The clothes, the setting, the evidence, all matched what Marie had told him. Were these all coincidence? What other explanation could there be? How else could he account for the faded name written at the foot of the paper?

Marie of Larzat.

Freddie sank to his knees, still clutching the sheet of paper. And, for the first time since the death of his brother, he began to weep. For George, for Marie, for all those who lay forgotten in the cold earth.

Chapter Eighteen

Everything was white.

When Freddie opened his eyes he saw the anxious faces of his friends looking down at him. White faces, white walls, white sheets on the bed.

He struggled to sit up. 'Where? Where am I?'

'In the hospital, old chap.' Brown used the formal voice he always put on when worried.

For a moment, Freddie couldn't work out anything. He looked down and saw his hands were bandaged. There was a dressing on his head too. He could feel the tightness of the bandage. His throat was sore, as if he had been shouting.

'How do you feel?' asked Turner. 'You were in quite a bad way when they brought you in. Feverish, muttering about ghosts.'

'They found the address of our

boarding house in Quillan in your pocket,' Brown added. 'That's how they knew where to find us.'

'Wasn't like you not to turn up without a word. When we didn't hear from you, we telephoned your hotel. Lucky, really. The owner remembered you were intending to take the mountain road to meet us.'

Little by little, his memories started to surface. 'Mr Galy? But he has no telephone.'

His friends exchanged a look. 'We spoke to the hotel owner in Foix,' Turner said.

Freddie didn't understand. 'No, that's not right,' he said. His voice was weak.

'You're getting muddled, old chap. You arrived in Foix on Sunday. Yesterday. Then this morning, Monday, you set off to drive to meet us in Quillan,' Brown said. 'But you never arrived. Don't you remember?'

Freddie leaned back on the white pillows. Still Monday? This made no sense. He stayed in Larzat last night, not Foix. He had spent the night talking with Marie.

'I remember the accident,' he said slowly. 'Car went off the road. That was Monday.'

'Exactly,' said Brown. He sounded relieved. 'You crashed. It was awful weather. It seems you left your car to find help and somehow lost your way. You were found in the mountains.'

Freddie frowned. The action made his head hurt. The bandage pulled at his skin.

'But today is Tuesday,' he said. 'I went to Larzat to find help. Mrs Galy arranged everything. The car is in the garage being fixed.'

This time, there was no mistaking the look of concern on Brown's face. 'They found the car at the side of the road, old chap. The front was all bashed in. Still there, for all I know.'

Turner took up the story. 'You were lucky. Tree stopped you from going over. People go missing for days. As it happens, a local fellow came upon your car at about three o'clock this afternoon. No sign of you. He was trying to decide what to do, when he saw something up above the road. He couldn't see if it was a man or a woman. Only that they were wearing a heavy red coat and were calling for help. He went up and found you inside one of the caves. You were out cold, with a nasty knock on your head. You were muttering something about a girl called Marie.'

A wave of memory washed through Freddie's mind. He closed his eyes.

'Bring us home,' he murmured.

'Rather grisly, though, as it happens,' Brown was saying. 'Of all the places to pick, you blundered into some sort of tomb. There were four bodies in there. Been there for some time. Hundreds of years, they are saying.'

Freddie remembered his lunch in the square. Surely that was Tuesday? He remembered climbing up and finding the rocks piled high in the narrow tunnel. He remembered seeing the four skeletons and the name on the parchment.

His eyes snapped wide open. 'The papers?' he said urgently. 'Are they safe?'

'Steady on, old chap,' Brown muttered.

A nurse swept towards the bed. 'If you upset my patient, gentlemen,' she said in a sharp voice, 'I shall ask you to leave.'

Turner held up his hand. 'Of course, of course.'

'Did you find the papers?' Freddie hissed, not caring if she told him off. He had to know.

Brown glanced over his shoulder. 'They are safe. You were hanging on to them for dear life, saying the girl's name over and over. You kept on about some date, or so the fellow said.'

Freddie sighed. He remembered: 1328.

'Turns out to be rather a coup, in fact,' Brown carried on. 'They will do tests, of course, but it seems the skeletons are very old indeed. It appears that during the wars of the Middle Ages, around here whole villages took shelter in the caves. Many of the bodies were never found. Those papers might turn out to be a hugely important find. The author had recorded the names of all those who fled to the mountain, and all those who stayed behind to defend the village.'

'The Galys, Michel Auty and his sons, the Marty sisters,' murmured Freddie. He could not explain it, but he was beginning to understand. None of them existed, although once they had. All those living and breathing people had been dead for some six hundred years.

'And so, here we are,' Turner said

brightly. 'You were brought to the hospital. They found our names and address in your pocket and got in touch. We drove here as soon as we could.'

Freddie let out a deep breath. 'And it is still only Monday, you say.'

'Coming up for midnight.'

'We should leave you to get some sleep,' Brown said.

Freddie heard the concern behind his words and was touched by it.

'Don't worry about a thing. We'll square it with the garage. We'll take care of things. You just think about getting back on your feet. You can't be too careful with a bump on the head.'

The nurse was hovering in her crisp uniform and stiff white cap. 'That's enough now, gentlemen.'

They stood up. Brown slapped him on the shoulder. Turner went to shake his hand, then thought better of it.

'We'll be back tomorrow,' he said. 'See how you're doing.'

Brown leaned down. 'And this girl, this Marie, the one you kept talking about.' He looked awkward. 'If you need me to help in any way, money, anything.' He tapped the side of his nose. 'Just say the word.'

Freddie smiled. He realised Brown thought he had got himself mixed up in some difficult love affair. In his clumsy way, he was trying to be a good friend.

He shook his head. 'Not to worry,' he said softly. 'She's long gone.'

'Jolly good.' Brown sighed with relief. 'Good. Very wise, very wise.'

The door swung shut behind them. The nurse returned a few minutes later to tuck him up for the night. Then she, too, left.

At last, Freddie was alone.

Around him, he heard the sounds of the hospital. The squeak of wheels somewhere in a distant corridor. The rubber-soled shoes of the night nurses going to and fro.

He knew he would never speak of this day. No one would believe him. Freddie did not know how it had happened. Nor why it had happened. He only knew that, for a moment, he had somehow slipped between the cracks in time. And in that instant, between reality and shadow, Marie had come to him. She had sought his help and he had given it.

Was she a ghost?

Perhaps. He thought of the way he had felt hidden eyes on his back as he walked through the woods. He closed his eyes. Marie had asked him to bring their bodies home. She had led him to the cave.

He had kept his word.

Six months later

October 1928

An English country garden in October. It was a late summer of warm sun and long days. The world was bathed in the colours of autumn, gold and copper, the deep green of the fir trees.

Wine-coloured leaves were scattered over the grass. Freddie stood with his hands clasped in front of him and his head bowed. His parents stood beside him. Their local parish priest, an old family friend, stood a little to one side.

Freddie had motored down to his childhood home the evening before. He was due back in town later to meet an editor at a leading publishing house. After his return from France, Freddie had started writing short pieces on French history and travel articles for the newspapers. From time to time, he wrote something more hard-hitting about war or grief or death. The editor had written last week and suggested Freddie might like to put them together into a book.

On the strength of it, Freddie had handed in his notice at the school. He was no longer content to spend his life in a job he didn't much like. Since his experiences in France, he was a new man. He wanted to do things, to make his time matter.

Freddie turned to his parents in turn and smiled. All that, a new career, writing, a break with the past, belonged to tomorrow. Today belonged to George. It was 20 October, George's birthday. He had finally persuaded his parents to accept that George would never be found. But it did not mean they could not remember him.

In front of them stood a simple headstone carved out of grey marble. Shining, bright, the sun glinted off the surface and sent rainbow patterns on to the thick grass. They had chosen the place where George had played as a boy, beneath the trees where the robins and the blackbirds made their nests.

The lettering was plain, giving George's name, his date of birth and the month and year of his death. They had never known exactly when he fell. Beneath that, carved in block capital letters, was a simple message.

'We shall not forget.'

At a nod from Freddie, the priest stepped forward and said a few words. He told stories of George as a boy, and described the courage with which he had gone to war and the tragedy of his death. Beside Freddie, his mother sobbed. He reached out and took her hand.

The priest made the sign of the cross and said the final words of blessing.

'Amen.'

He stood back. Freddie looked to his father, who gave a brief shake of his head. His mother looked up at him and nodded. He squeezed her hand, then let go.

As he stepped forward, he was thinking of Marie's gravestone and those of her family in the tiny cemetery in France. Their names, too, would now not be forgotten. History is words carved on stone so that we should remember. Words endure when memories fade into dust.

'Welcome home, George,' he said.

In the branches of the tree above his head, the robin began to sing.